THE SCARLETT CURSE

The Sacred Blade of Profanity series
Book I

Written by Toneye Eyenot

Edited by: J. Ellington Ashton Press Staff
Cover Art by: David McGlumphy

http://jellingtonashton.com/
Copyright.
Toneye Eyenot
©2015, Toneye Eyenot
ALL RIGHTS RESERVED. This book contains material protected under International and Federal Copyright Laws and Treaties. Any unauthorized reprint or use of this material is prohibited. No part of this book, including the cover and photos, may be reproduced or transmitted in any form or by any means, electronic or mechanical, including photocopying, recording, or by any information storage and retrieval system without express written permission from the author / publisher. All rights reserved.

Any resemblance to persons, places living or dead is purely coincidental.
This is a work of fiction.

This book is dedicated to Scarlett Letta, who set me on this journey...Thank You.

Also, to my Good Friends & Family who have inspired, helped and encouraged me in my first foray into this field of Horrors. You were all instrumental in guiding me through and especially out of a very dark two years. Eye am humbled and eternally grateful. O, how the past returns to the present and opens a multitude of futures before One!

Very special thanks to my Mum and Dad, my Son Odin, my beautiful Jenni, my Metal Brothers... Jim, Tony, Mark...and of korpse, my Metal Sister, Sandeye. Couldn't have got to this point without each and every one of you!

*Yours,
Toneye Eyenot*

Another time…Place…Indeed, another reality akin to our own. The fates of many have fallen and will yet fall under the ethereal eye and insatiable bloodlust of The Sacred Blade Of Profanity. Scarlett's centuries long struggle with The Blade Of Power begins to take its toll. Thousands have perished at the hands of Scarlett and The Sacred Blade, as will many thousands more in the centuries to follow…Or perhaps not? An innocent child, who unwittingly holds the secret to The Blades' demise, just may change everything… But who will suffer most?

Chapter 1

Secretly and with great stealth, Scarlett drew her silver, razor-sharp dagger. The handle, encrusted with amethyst and moonstone, nestled perfectly in her comfortable yet strong grip.

It would seem as if its ancient architect had her very hand in mind when fashioning such Beauty and Power.

The Sacred Blade Of Profanity had, indeed, harnessed vast landscapes of Power in the course of its immeasurable existence. It had been in her possession now for longer than she remembered. Its very nature transcended time and space, and in what seems like many centuries... many lifetimes, Scarlett would forever marvel at its unique ability to carry its possessor, unaffected by the cruelty of time. For as long as she kept the Blade by her flesh, Scarlett was, by all accounts, somewhat immortal.

"What do you intend to do with that?" A booming, authoritative voice behind her startled Scarlett. It also gained the attention of everybody in the crowded section of market, where her intended prey stood anxiously by a stall of hats. His nervous disposition was inflicted upon him by the close proximity of the Sacred Blade, and by Scarlett's single-minded intent to end his existence in this world. The old man could not fathom why he was suddenly overcome with such dread, as he tried on, in the most awkward and clumsy way, nearly every item of headwear.

Joshua Melkerin was never one to wear a hat. His head was simply too large, and an odd, hat unfriendly shape. At this moment, however, Joshua had the overwhelming urge to hide his face... to conceal his identity.

He was certain that nobody was aware of his most recent debauchery. Nor was anyone aware of how long he had been carrying his secret around with him. But The Sacred Blade Of Profanity knew. Oh, it knew too well—and it craved Joshua's profanity as the wolf does the lamb.

"Well?" impatiently inquired the now irate voice.

Scarlett didn't flinch, but kept her eyes fixed on Joshua Melkerin, who was also startled by the sudden loud voice. So much so, that it caused him to drop his most recent choice to the dirt at his feet and stare at Scarlett, his mouth opening and closing in a mixture of fear, outrage, and humiliation at his clumsiness.

The stallholder swiftly spoke up, and insisted that the beret was now the property of this fumbling gentleman.

"Look at it! How can I sell this now? You have ruined it!"

The old man became so flustered by this very public embarrassment, that he turned a little too quickly back to face the stallholder, and in doing so, sent the entire collection of hats tumbling into the filthy street.

All of this happened in a matter of moments - more than enough time for Scarlett to assess the situation and act accordingly. The Blade, with its immunity to the constraints of time and space, carried across to Scarlett the ability to act instantly and without hesitation. She casually turned to the now distracted man behind her... a town official, no less, and silently ran the keen edge of her Dagger across his throat as she walked away through the confused crowd.

Scarlett was gone before the man even realised his throat was slit, and the front of his tunic suddenly became a dark shade of crimson. His knees buckled beneath him—a woman screamed, followed by a mass of shouts and panic.

These events were already a distant memory to Scarlett as she slipped, unnoticed, through the town gates, and made her way back to her forest home.

* * *

The thirst had only been minutely sated though. To retain its full potential...its absolute Power, The Sacred Blade Of Profanity demanded, like an unruly child, full immersion. It demanded deep, penetrating wounds. It needed to feel the blood, still living and warm, blanketing its cold metal frame. A quick taste of throat flesh merely excited the Blade and aroused its bloodlust beyond imagination.

Scarlett knew she now had very little linear time left to give the Blade its fill. The memories of past failings were still very painful indeed. The scar beneath her right breast throbbed violently, and the pain in her lung was almost crippling. Scarlett couldn't go home just yet. She had to turn back. There was simply no other option.

The entire town of Mills Wall had erupted into an unspeakable hysteria. Apart from the recent disappearances of several of the town's children, Mills Wall was a peaceful, friendly town. Everybody knew everybody's business, but that never seemed to be cause for trouble. The missing children, however, had upset the townsfolk considerably, and understandably so.

Never, in the history of Mills Wall, had such a tragic sequence of events occurred. Of course, there was the occasional neighbourly dispute, but these were invariably solved with minimal fuss or trouble. The countryside where the town was situated had always been believed to be a place of harmonious energies. Perhaps this is why Scarlett has spent so many years in the one spot.

Though she rarely interacted with the locals, this place had felt like Home for a very, very long time.

*** * * ***

Gagging on saliva and blood, Noel could do nothing but lay helpless in the dirt and watch as people ran past and all around him, shouting and screaming in a most ridiculous panic. He was a large, strong man. Close to seven feet tall, he was military trained, though his training hadn't been needed for some time. As he lay there, he couldn't help but wonder how such a slight creature as that mysterious woman could have slipped past his guard so easily and, in the process, manage to render him effectively useless. Perhaps it had simply been too long since his training had served any kind of real purpose.

His eyes watered profusely, and his nostrils filled with dust, kicked up by the scores of feet scampering this way and that. His final thoughts were of gratitude to the gentle hands of a woman who lifted his spinning head off the cold, hard ground and cradled it in her lap. He had neither the strength, nor the care, really, to protest against the woman using her coarse garment to apply pressure to his fatal wound. Her vain attempt to halt the copious flow of his lifeblood only served to suffocate him more thoroughly. Noel Hartren, Sergeant of Mills Wall

Town Guard, passed from this world in a whirlwind of chaos and confusion.

Chapter 2

In the midst of this confusion, Joshua Melkerin still stood, dumbfounded by the events that had unfolded before him. The stallholder, who had just lost most of his stock due to Joshua's cumbersome mishap, was no longer concerned, as he rushed forward to aid the fallen official. Joshua, still dazed as if in a terrible dream, stumbled off into the failing sun, towards his home.

"How does she know?" he asked himself. "Does she know?" Joshua quickened his pace, muttering to himself all the way. "Maybe she is a child's mother? An older sibling, perhaps?"

A man walking towards him looked up, expecting to see two people engaging in conversation. He quickly jumped aside as the seemingly delirious Joshua rushed past him, completely oblivious and babbling like an idiot.

"Who was she? Those eyes! They burned right through my poor soul!" Joshua ruminated verbally as he walked.

As he neared the end of the darkening street, Joshua stopped for a moment and leaned against a wall to catch his breath. He was sweating profusely, and not just because of his fast pace and ailing health. He closed his eyes as he wiped his brow with his sleeve, and there she was—staring! In her hand, a dagger that screamed his name, sending chills through his entire body. Joshua opened his eyes... a moment of sheer terror. He expected to see his assassin standing before him, but no...

The quiet street was now empty, and in the seconds that he had closed his eyes it seemed to have become considerably darker. Joshua resumed his urgent rush home. Only minutes away now.

"What if she's there...waiting in the shadows? Inside my home, even! *Who was she?*"

His own voice frightened him as it echoed through the narrow street, bouncing from wall to wall, to road and all around him...the echoes of a madman.

"Ha! They'll think it was her! The witch! Hahaha!! I must get home."

* * *

"So...tired..."

Scarlett spoke with a sigh in her soft voice, as she often did, to nobody in particular. She preferred her own company rather than that of fools. Throughout her long, sometimes tedious, but often dramatic life, she had certainly crossed paths with her fair share. More often than not, such meetings would end somewhat badly, and usually tragically, for these miserable creatures. Her reminding scar and the agonising throb had now subsided. The Sacred Blade Of Profanity had 'made its point', so to speak.

Scarlett had been weakened considerably by its infuriated attack on her psyche however, and she would have given anything in that moment to lay where she stood and sleep for an eternity.

But no, the Blade would not allow rest or respite until it had fed. The symbiotic relationship between Scarlett and The Sacred Blade Of Profanity was so profoundly entwined, in that whilst the Blade was an instrument and a source of incredible Power, it was Scarlett's own immovable will that kept the Blade in its empowered state.

Just as an injured or threatened wild beast, it would strike mercilessly, if need be, in its fight for self-preservation. She had changed her course, and now returned to finish the appointed task at hand.

This task had taken on a terrible new burden though. She had been seen by a substantial portion of the townsfolk, and the slaughter of Joshua Melkerin would now be no simple task to undertake. He had stared into the eyes of his demise, and was now fully aware of the source of his sudden, seemingly unfounded onset of nervousness and dread. Scarlett felt the excitement in The Blade Of Power at the prospect of spilling the blood of many to get to Joshua. The Sacred Blade Of Profanity would feast heartily tonight, it seemed.

* * *

"Don't stray too far, Dera. Dusk turns to night and all manner of wild beast abound. Stay within my sight."

Phenoluh Harke struggled to keep up with her young daughter as she ran ahead into the failing light. Dera Harke was a handful, to put it mildly, always had been, ever since her impatient journey from womb to world. Dera was fortunate to have such an understanding mother as Phenoluh. The world she knew was a constant source of excitement and wonder.

At eleven years old, Dera had never spoken a single word. Whether it was by choice, or she was simply incapable, Phenoluh was still unsure. She had caught Dera on quite a few occasions humming strange tunes to something that wasn't there. Melodies and airs that were completely unfamiliar to Phenoluh.

Dera lived in her own secret world. *"Off with the fairies"* the townsfolk would say in their private conversations, but never in Dera or Phenoluh's presence.

Scarlett, also walking in her own world, didn't see the child suddenly appear out of the darkness. Her hand reached instinctively for the Dagger. Fortunately for Dera, not quickly enough. Dera loved to run as fast as her skinny little legs could carry her through the pitch of night. She often ran for hours, much to the dismay of her mother, who was loath to turn her back for even an instant. The collision was sudden and shocking for both Dera and Scarlett, as they fell in a heap on the soft earth. Soft though it may have been, the impact was enough for Scarlett. In her weakened state, she hit the ground hard, and saw the darkness become darker, until she quickly saw and felt nothing at all.

After some moments, Dera recovered and peered into the face of the beautiful stranger who lay unconscious before her. Out of the corner of her eye, Dera caught the gleam of The Sacred Blade Of Profanity. Their chance meeting had sent the Blade from Scarlett's tired hand, and it lay partially hidden in a tuft of grass.

"Hello?" Dera whispered in a barely audible voice. "Hello? Are you ok?"

The woman remained motionless and without reply. The dagger by her limp hand seemed to dance with light, and just as Phenoluh emerged from the darkness, Dera quickly snatched up The Sacred Blade, and tucked it under her belt.

"Child, you'll be the death of me. Hello? What's happened

here?"

The child looked up at her mother as a single tear ran down her cheek. Phenoluh reached down to pick up her daughter, and froze as she saw Scarlett more clearly, laying there, out cold. The woman from the marketplace!

"Dera, are you hurt, dear?" Phenoluh inquired of her daughter caringly.

Dera shook her head, looked down at Scarlett's peaceful form, then back to Phenoluh and again at Scarlett.

"What happened, Dera?"

Dera clapped her hands together and threw them out wide to describe the collision with the mysterious woman. Dera's eyes pleaded with Phenoluh as she looked from her mother to Scarlett and back again. Phenoluh carefully stood Dera back on the ground and knelt by Scarlett, checking for breathing or any other signs of life.

"You're a hard little lass to have knocked this poor woman unconscious! Did you do this?"

Dera nodded, sheepishly. She was a tough child. Her refusal to talk had gotten her into countless scuffles in the schoolyard with vicious children who took pleasure in mistreating those who were 'different'. It didn't take many group beatings before Dera began to fight back, and fight back she most certainly did! This had a double-edged advantage for her. On one hand, the beatings quickly ceased. On the other, the children at school were now frightened of Dera, and steered well clear of her in the playground. Which was just how she liked it.

Her social skills weren't exactly her strong point. Nor did she care for them to be. Dera had plenty of friends where she spent most of her time.

"Well, she isn't dead," chuckled Phenoluh, as she tried to sit Scarlett up. "You really did do a number on her though."

Dera hung her head in mock shame and hid the smile that played on her lips. She managed to push out another tear, as she looked up at her mother, and once again at the beautiful stranger.

"We can't leave her here. She'll be food for the wolves before daybreak. You will help me look after her, child. After all, it was you who left her in this sorry way."

Phenoluh squatted in front of Scarlett as Dera lifted the limp arms over her mother's strong shoulders. Phenoluh stood up with

Scarlett slumped over her back and began walking towards their cottage. It was a fair journey, as their home was nestled in the beginnings of the forest trees, about half a mile from town. A multitude of conflicting thoughts and scenarios played out in Phenoluh's head as she stepped carefully through the dark, the surprisingly light Scarlett on her back.

Dera was dancing circles around them as they approached their humble little home.

This woman will be sought after by the town's guard, Phenoluh thought to herself. *What am I thinking, bringing her here? Dera's life could be in danger, as could my own.*

Dera seemed to pick up on her mother's troubled thoughts and quickly came to her side. She hugged Phenoluh's leg tightly, which made walking a difficult chore indeed.

"Dera, child! Please! Do you want me to drop her? You have already caused this poor dear enough harm! Now, run ahead and get the door. Good girl."

The little girl was off like a shot towards the cottage, reaching the gate in a matter of moments. She burst through the door, barely stopping to open it, and crouched down to feed the fireplace. With The Sacred Blade Of Profanity still tucked in her belt, Dera felt something she had never before known. A darkness washed over her like a wave of putrid blood. It was both exhilarating and horrifying at once.

Dera didn't know whether to run back outside into the night, or sit still by the fire and wait for her mother to arrive. She opted for sitting still, though on the inside she was reaching a crescendo of scarcely contained excitement, mixed with untold horror, that froze her to the spot.

Phenoluh was out of breath as she entered the warmth of the cottage and carefully laid Scarlett on her bed. The whole while, Dera stared at her mother.

Confusion addled Dera's young brain as she struggled to retain the deep love she had for the woman who raised her, alone. All that Dera knew of her father was that he was a hunter, fallen foul of his prey. She was barely two years old when her mother received the tragic news, and Dera had since lost all memory of those first two years of life with both father and mother.

Phenoluh was her rock. She relied on her for most everything, although, at a glance, one would not think so. Even to her own mother,

Dera Harke gave had an air of someone completely independent of anyone.

The thoughts that clouded Dera's mind now were not those she was used to thinking. She began to wonder who this woman, who selflessly gave her everything she needed, really was.

"Chiiild..."

The voice sounded like it was all around her, yet coming from within. Its gender was not discernible, but its intentions, its tone, certainly were. Dera sat rigidly by the fire, continuing to stare silently at Phenoluh while the voice continued.

"This woman brings great danger to your home, Dera." the voice said, solemnly.

"How do you know my name?"

Phenoluh sat bolt upright as a chill raced up her spine and made her hair stand on end. Her little girl had spoken!

Dera's voice brought tears to Phenoluh's eyes as she turned to see her daughter staring at her with a cold, blank expression on her face. Phenoluh's heart sank as she realised exactly what Dera had said. Her name? Who was she speaking to? Or more frighteningly...who was speaking to Dera?

"Child? Sweetheart? Who were you talking to just now?" Phenoluh questioned, as she rose slowly to her feet and cautiously approached the little girl, who had seemingly forgotten who she was looking at. The overwhelming sense of dread that had caused poor Joshua Melkerin such an embarrassing public scene, now clutched at Phenoluh's chest. Dera was definitely not herself. She began to rock slightly. She tilted her head unnaturally, and watched inquisitively as this increasingly unknown and menacing person advanced towards her.

"Dera?"

Each step became increasingly difficult, like wading through a swamp. Phenoluh was beginning to feel real terror now, as her child continued to act in a way that she'd never seen.

Her maternal instinct, however, pushed her forward, step by agonizing step. Her little girl... all she had left in this harsh life... was in some sort of terrible danger.

"She means you harm, Dera. She sent this woman to capture you in your nightly excursions through the woods. They will make you a prisoner, and I have not the heart to tell you what they have planned for you. You must strike now.... Take me in your hand, child. I will do

the rest."

The voice was sweetly bewitching to Dera. She became convinced that Phenoluh and the mysterious woman from the forest were indeed going to do terrible things to her. Why? She was a good girl. She didn't deserve to be held captive, or worse! Just who was this ugly person coming towards her? Of course, somewhere in there, Dera knew exactly who it was. Her rational mind, however, had taken a back seat in this macabre pantomime.

"Dera, darling, what's wrong?" A cold sweat broke out all over Phenoluh's body, and she fought the urge to vomit. Every fibre of her being screamed at her to run, as fast and as far away as she possibly could, but her beautiful little Dera needed her. She would gladly give up her life before abandoning her baby.

"Dera?"

"Mother."

The look of fear and confusion on Dera's face as she spoke to Phenoluh for the first time in her life pushed all other concerns aside - Phenoluh rushed forward and scooped up her precious little girl in a tight embrace. Her body shook with sobs, while tears streamed down her face as she held Dera tightly.

"Mother."

Dera sighed and plunged The Sacred Blade of Profanity up under Phenoluh's ribs. Phenoluh gasped in agony as she lost her grip on Dera and dropped to her knees. The trigger had been pulled, and The Blade came alive in the young child's hand. Dera leapt onto Phenoluh, growling like a wild beast as she stabbed and slashed maniacally into her mother's neck and chest. Blood sprayed into Dera's eyes and onto her tongue, driving her into a complete frenzy. The morbid duet of Dera's desperate cries to stop what she was doing mingled with the hysterical laughter of The Blade... the resulting cacophony rang out through the still of night.

* * *

The freezing water began crushing Scarlett as she desperately tried to swim upwards. Her clothing wrapped and tangled around her tired arms and legs, only to drag her deeper into the murky cold. There was something missing, though she couldn't, for the life of her, figure out what it was. All Scarlett could do was continue her losing battle, or succumb to her death. She could hear what sounded like cries, or maybe screams... Although they were muffled, there was also a certain clarity that indicated to Scarlett that they came from the surface of what was looking to be her watery grave.

What was missing? Although her clothes were weighing her down and making escape impossible, Scarlett felt strangely naked. The thought made her suddenly burst into laughter, which resounded all around her as if she were in a great hall, and not in the final moments of drowning within a ravenous and suffocating body of water.

The clarity in the muffled cries above reached down to Scarlett, gently eased her mind, and the panicked struggling ceased. Calmly, Scarlett began to remove her cumbersome garb. All the while, she kept her focus on the dim light above which finally seemed to be getting closer. She held no regard for each item of clothing she let loose to sink into the cold darkness. Her single-minded attention was on the light and soothing cries from above. With nothing left but her undergarments, Scarlett easily rose to the surface, and as she broke the water, what awaited her would sicken her to her very core.

Scarlett sat up abruptly, gasping for the precious air she had seemingly been robbed of. Instead of a watery surface though, Scarlett was met by a vision so terrible, she instinctively tried to get back below the water. There was no water. Just a very comfortable bed in a room she had never been in, and a little girl, completely red, staring inches from her face. Scarlett backed away on the bed, and the little girl sat down slowly. For what seemed like hours, the two sat and silently stared. It was then that the naked feeling of Scarlett's dream became apparent. The Sacred Blade Of Profanity had found its way into the little girl's hand! Scarlett's immediate reaction to this bloody sight was to frantically check herself for wounds. Her relief was marred by the sudden realisation that there was a lifeless body over by the fireplace, mutilated beyond reason, and surrounded by a still expanding pool of blood. Dera turned The Sacred Blade Of Profanity toward herself, and for an instant Scarlett was sure the massacre was about to continue.

"My mother is dead."

Dera bowed her head and handed the blood-soaked knife to Scarlett.

These were to be the last conscious words Dera would utter for the rest of her life. Scarlett wanted to cry, to scream at the top of her lungs. How did this happen? How did she come to be in this cottage with a young child who had just butchered her own mother with The Sacred Blade Of Profanity? The Blade which had given her the highest joys and the deepest misery?

The child seemed catatonic. She didn't move or look up. She didn't sob or even seem overly upset. She just sat on the end of the bed with her head down. Scarlett had killed many people in her time, easily into the several thousands. The Blade demanded its regular gluttonous bloodfeast, and Scarlett had long ago detached and desensitised herself from her victims and their experiences. It was the only way her sanity could remain intact. But as the events of the previous hour unfolded in her mind, Scarlett became violently ill. The stench of blood and fresh death, coupled with the sight of an innocent child covered head to toe in her own mother's blood, overwhelmed her.

Scarlett saw through the ethereal eye of The Sacred Blade as if she stood over Dera, guiding her hand with every stab and hack. She felt each penetration, felt Phenoluh's disbelief and agonising terror, as if it were her own child screaming in both deranged joy and absolute dismay as she viciously drove The Blade in again, and again, and again...

Chapter 3

As he reached the door to his house, Joshua Melkerin was a bundle of frayed nerves. He took the key in his trembling hand and dropped it as he tried to fit it into the keyhole. He was almost certain the demon from the marketplace would come for him tonight, and was at a complete loss as to how he was going to survive to see another sunrise. Opening the door might well be his last act on earth. He pressed his ear up against the door.

"Is she inside already?"

The silence of an uninhabited dwelling sounded through the solid wood, which relieved him slightly.

The dread feeling was still with him, but only residually. Nothing like what he felt moments before making eye contact with his would-be killer. As he bent to pick up his key, a dog trotted past in the street. Startled, Joshua lurched forward, smashing his head into the door.

"Fuck! Dammit! Pull yourself together, Joshua! The witch is not here. Get inside and bolt the door before you take your own life by misadventure, you clumsy fool!"

Once inside, and with the door securely locked, Joshua was able to relax just a little. He had been gone for hours, and there was one more thing to be taken care of before he could retire for the night. An elaborate portrait of his Great Grandfather Pellegrin Melkerin hung on the wall, exactly halfway down the hallway. Joshua tilted the picture from the bottom corner to reveal a lever inside the wall. He pulled the lever and a door opened a few steps along. A single cough escaped the hidden chamber, and Joshua descended the stairs, into the dark room below. Four children sat huddled together in the furthest corner of the empty room, the cold stone floor offering no comfort. Not a scrap of furniture or bedding. Just a large, cold, bare room.

"Up!"

Joshua's voice boomed throughout the chamber. Immediately, three of the four children stood and helped the fourth child, who could have been no older than six or seven.

"This will not do," Joshua muttered under his breath. There were still three whole days before the traders would pass through town again. Four were promised to them, and a strong, healthy four. The young one looked very poorly. His hair was plastered to his face with sweat, and his mouth hung open loosely. He seemed to have some trouble breathing. Joshua was furious. This one had to go. He could not chance the others acquiring the illness. This meant he must now find a replacement within three days, and somehow discard the weak one. With the events of the afternoon, not to mention the townsfolk now keeping a very close eye on their children and viewing even their closest friends with suspicion, this would prove tricky.

"Leave him," says Joshua. "He will come with me. He is not your concern now."

The children obeyed without protest, as they stepped away from the young boy, who proceeded to double over in a coughing fit. They stood in a short line as Joshua went from child to child. He peered into their frightened eyes as he roughly moved their heads from side to side, checking for signs of illness. They seemed fit enough. Without another word, Joshua picked up the sick boy, carrying him under his arm up the steps.

As the door slammed shut and the room again fell into pitch darkness, the remaining three children carefully felt their way across the floor, into their little corner, and huddled together once more. Not a word was spoken between them. The terror had fixed their tongues, and all they could do was wonder in fear about the fate that awaited their young cellmate.

Young Ander shivered uncontrollably as he watched Joshua pace back and forth, deep in troubled thought. The cold sweat clung to his pallid skin and felt like a fine layer of ice that chilled him to the bone. The fever had only taken hold mere hours earlier, but its rapid onset had left Ander weak, disoriented, and exhausted. He still had no idea where he was, or why he had been taken from his home. The other children in the cellar below were just as frightened and confused. The last thing any of them remembered was being tucked into a warm bed and kissed goodnight by loving parents, only to wake in freezing cold darkness on a hard stone floor with the most terrible headaches.

Ander hadn't had that luxury, however. His father was a cruel, harsh man. He demanded complete servitude from his wife and four children, and did not hesitate to beat any of them mercilessly if his demands weren't followed to the letter. Ander had run away that evening, as his father 'punished' his older sister for just such an infringement. He usually fell asleep under the giant oak that grew just outside the grounds of his home. This was where he spent many a cold, hungry night. He would curl up at the roots of the great tree and dread the consequences of returning to face his father in the morning. In a strange way, he somehow felt safer in his new prison.

Joshua stopped pacing and stared at the floor for several moments. Ander could now identify his captor, and would surely run his mouth. He can't return the boy, nor can he put him back with the other three. Not to mention the woman from the market with the blade that screamed for his blood. He knew it was a matter of very little time before he would have her to deal with again. This must be rectified as soon as possible. He looked up at the young lad and their eyes met. Joshua looked away quickly - that desperate, questioning gaze was too much for his guilty conscience to bear.

"What is your name, boy?" Joshua asked.

As Ander tried to speak his name to the foreboding hulk of a man, Joshua quickly spun around and let his knuckles crack soundly across the side of the young boy's face. The force sent the tiny child airborne in what seemed like slow motion. Ander felt the familiar sting of knuckle, though this time a lot harder than what he was used to. His body had become light and his mind dark. Ander slipped out of consciousness before his little body hit the floor.

Joshua quickly scooped Ander up and rushed towards the back of the house. The grounds behind were well tended by Joshua. He had several patches of loose soil where he grew some of the finest vegetables in all of Mills Wall. Nobody knew the secret to his extravagantly sized produce, with a taste that would bring vendors from all the surrounding towns to his home.

Perhaps it was something in his composting technique? One could only guess...

Joshua briskly rolled the boy tight in an old, worn blanket, and once again picked up the limp form, continuing out to the back.

Grabbing the shovel by the back door, he made his way through the gardens to the centre patch. He had harvested a very healthy yield this season from this very patch, which was now bare. He dropped the boy and began to dig frantically.

Ander, stunned back into consciousness by the sudden thud on the ground, was horrified to find himself unable to move and barely able to breathe. He struggled in near hysteria, and screamed as loud as his fever stricken lungs would allow. Without a second thought, Joshua turned around and unceremoniously drove the blade of the shovel down hard. The bundle near his feet fell silent, as young Ander's head became separate from his now weakly twitching body. Joshua turned back to continue with his gruesome task.

* * *

"Your name is Dera, yes?" asked Scarlett, who had not the slightest clue how she knew this. The words just fell, involuntarily, from her mouth. Dera nodded slightly, then looked up at Scarlett. The blood of her dead mother, now crusted on her soft skin, gave her the appearance of a creature from the foulest depths of Hell.

Dera held no expression and spoke not a word, simply staring vacantly at Scarlett, causing her to recoil involuntarily. Scarlett felt fear for the first time in her long memory. This was her doing. Her failure in the marketplace to keep her task from the knowledge of the townsfolk had led to this tragic outcome. The Sacred Blade Of Profanity thrived on the blood of the profane, the guilty—those who had forfeited their right to life.

Phenoluh Harke was a good person, a loving mother and friendly neighbour, always willing to be of service to any in need, and never prone to judge. The Sacred Blade Of Profanity had taken the life of an innocent in the most brutal and vicious manner. In the process, it had also succeeded in taking the innocence of a child, and showing her the darkest horrors of human capability. Dera had been irreversibly changed, and Scarlett took the entire burden of blame upon herself.

In a sudden onset of rage, Scarlett hurled The Blade across the room. The loud thud of The Dagger into the back of the solid wooden chair knocked the wind out of her, and the resounding clatter as it fell to the floor made her hold her head as she released an agonising wail. Dera scrambled immediately across the floor and reverently picked up the weapon. She slowly approached Scarlett, who held her head still in her trembling hands, sobbing with pain. Dera carefully wiped the blood from The Blade, and as much from the elaborately designed handle as she was able to, before kneeling at Scarlett's feet and gently placing The Sacred Blade in her lap.

Scarlett immediately felt the agony drain from her body and mind, and looked up to see Dera gazing at her, with tears streaming haphazardly down her crusty, blood-stained cheeks. Dera now understood perfectly the scope of The Blade's Power and the hold it had on Scarlett. She also knew she was now bound to Scarlett and The Sacred Blade Of Profanity in a most disturbing way. Her mother was dead, and by her own hand! Dera recognised that she was alone in the world now. Even her friends unseen had seemed to retreat from her internal playground. She had never felt so isolated, so utterly alone.

Phenoluh's mutilated body had bled out, and lay in a twisted heap near the fireplace. Scarlett shifted across the bed to Dera, who sat looking at her dead mother with silent tears, and pulled her close in a comforting embrace. Dera was her responsibility now. Scarlett had never had children of her own, and was not accustomed to this feeling that took her. She didn't know what to say to Dera to ease her pain, so she just held the bloody child tightly to her, trying to decide her next move. Dera's little body shook lightly in silent sobs of grief and despair, and the tears welled up in Scarlett's eyes as she softly stroked the child's stiff, blood-crusted hair. She needed to remove the body and any trace of the macabre event that had transpired here.

Phenoluh was a large woman, and her dead weight would prove difficult to move. Dera became still as she rested her head against Scarlett's chest, soothed by the sound of her beating heart. The child had fallen into a nightmare sleep as she murmured unintelligible words and syllables. Scarlett slowly and carefully laid Dera down and covered her with a soft blanket, then sat, looking at Phenoluh's inert form.

The waning moon outside gave little light, but enough for Scarlett to be able to survey the surrounding night. She moved quickly and silently around the outside of the cottage, to the back. Thick with undergrowth, the forest behind would have to suffice as Phenoluh's temporary resting place. There was still much to do before the cover of darkness gave way to a new sun, and Scarlett was still fairly weakened by The Sacred Blade's vicious attacks, both on her own psyche, and on the innocent mother and child. This was a new development in her relationship with The Sacred Blade Of Profanity. Never, in the entire time she had carried it, had The Dagger so joyously taken the life of one undeserving.

Scarlett returned inside, looked over to Dera's sleeping form briefly, then to the corpse in the pool of congealed blood. A door leading to the woods at the back of the cottage gave Scarlett some relief. She wouldn't have to attempt to drag the dead body all the way around outside—a lot less effort and infinitely less mess. She braced herself as she gripped onto Phenoluh's ankles and began her slow struggle to the back door. It may as well have been a mile to the door, and Scarlett groaned in frustrated exertion.

This was going to take all night, and there was still the poor child to consider. Asleep on the bed, Dera was still caked in her mother's blood. It leached through into her sleep, and tormented her with nightmare visions of a screaming blade, and her mother's terrified face pleading silently with wide eyes for the horror to cease. Moving mere inches with each gargantuan effort, Scarlett slowly neared the back of the cottage.

The chill night air danced on the beads of sweat that ran down Scarlett's face. Ignorant of the sharp brambles that tore at the flesh of her hands, she desperately tried to conceal Phenoluh's lifeless bulk beneath the undergrowth. She was only a few metres from the rear of the cottage, but time had gotten away from her in her struggle to bring the body this far.

"This will have to do," Scarlett told herself out loud, as the darkness of night just began to give way ever so slightly. Soon the dawn would break, and the first stirrings of day life would begin. Even now, her position was visible to the town of Mills Wall, and to anyone awake who may chance to peer in her direction.

There were still the tasks of cleaning the bloody mess inside and covering the trail leading to Phenoluh's makeshift burial site. Dera still wore the evidence of matricide on her sleeping body. Something was truly amiss here. The Sacred Blade had never failed to make time Scarlett's ally; now, time played the taunting enemy with each passing moment. This feeling of haste, an extremely vague memory to Scarlett, was nonetheless a terribly uncomfortable sensation. She did not like it one bit.

Scarlett knew what was imminently nigh. It had been more than a lifetime now since she had performed The Ritual Of Cleansing, just as it had been performed more than a lifetime previous to that. How long, exactly, had she carried this burden? She honestly could not fathom.

The piercing, inhuman howl of anguish suddenly shattered her meandering thoughts as it ran through the misty pre-dawn stillness. Scarlett rushed back inside to find Dera sitting up on the bed. She clutched the blanket to her chest and stared at the bloody site where her mother had once lay. Dera suddenly turned her gaze to Scarlett as she entered the room, eyes wide with terror, like that of a frightened animal. She had awoken to find herself alone, which had never troubled her in her entire, short life. The nightmare reality had brought her fully into the now, and Dera again suffered that terrible feeling of loneliness, twisting her soul in despair and hopelessness. Scarlett hurried across the floor and took Dera in a tight embrace.

"I'm here, Dera. It's ok, little one. I won't leave you again, I promise."

Dera threw her arms around Scarlett and buried her face in her shoulder. Dera felt somewhat awkward, as she had never allowed anyone but her mother to touch her, let alone hold her in comfort. Scarlett, however, showed Dera genuine concern and even a slight, naively maternal instinct, which allowed Dera to relax a little, then a little more.

Rubbing her teary eyes on Scarlett's soft, hooded shawl, Dera let go in an outpouring of emotional devastation and gave herself to Scarlett, her new Protector.

If ever there was a time to say something to the child, it was at that very moment. Scarlett was lost for words. Her body shook involuntarily, fighting back her own sobs of grief and loss, which she shared with Dera, so as not to disturb the little girl. Her heart was broken and her soul shattered. Scarlett felt herself holding fast to secure her balance on the outer circle of the spiral out of control.

Chapter 4

With the young lad tucked neatly in his fresh garden grave, Joshua took a few moments to catch his breath.

"What a terrible shame," he said to the patted down earth in front of him. "Rest well, young man." Joshua turned and made his way back inside.

The remorse he felt for the young child was minimal in comparison to the growing apprehension that filled his being. This had been the easy task. With the better part of the night behind him, Joshua now had less than three days to replace the young boy. That is, if he were to survive that long.

The dread feeling once again began to build up inside his chest. The anxiety he was feeling clouded his tired mind, making it near impossible to formulate a strategy.

Joshua decided that perhaps just a few hours of rest might bring about some order to his thoughts. As he climbed the stairs to his bed chamber, the vision of the woman in the marketplace swirled around in his head. Sleep, it seems, won't come readily, but he must at least try.

"Tomorrow will be a busy day," Joshua reminded himself, which reinforced his need to have all of his wits about him. Every time he tried to arrange some sort of plan, however, The Sacred Blade Of Profanity would flood him with doubts and second guesses.

Joshua knew it was the demon and her dagger causing the disarray of his thoughts. He had no idea how he knew. He just did. The woman from the market wanted him dead. Her penetrating eyes left no doubt about that, and he knew she carried a knife that was by no means an ordinary dagger. She had come for him at the command of The Sacred Blade Of Profanity. He felt she had absolutely no say in the matter. A sudden feeling of sympathy and sadness for this woman, who was bound to take his life by any means, started to put perspective into his own role in this situation.

"Joshua Melkerin," he addressed himself out loud, "You sir, are a worm. You will get what you deserve for your transgressions."

The full realisation of the path he had taken was devastating to Joshua as he slumped down onto the end of his bed. The tears of self-pity that welled up in his eyes made the floor he was staring at move and dance in a mocking display. The most devastating aspect of his realisation though, was that he had no choice but to continue along this dark, evil road. He had come too far. He had passed the crossroads, and stumbled headlong into his own personal nightmare, from which there was no turning back.

* * *

Outside the cottage, the first birdsong heralded the new day. There was much to be done before Scarlett could take Dera and leave the child's home forever. Ever so gently, Scarlett released the girl from her embrace and stood up to begin the gruesome task of cleaning the mess of Phenoluh's blood from the floor and nearby wall. Dera sobbed quietly, as Scarlett went to fetch the bucket by the front door and then proceeded outside to the well, thankfully situated out of view of the nearby town. As she approached the well in the chill morning mist, Scarlett felt a presence behind her. She slowly, casually reached for The Sacred Blade and turned to see Dera standing, uneasily looking at the ground and swinging her arms from front to behind.

"You gave me a bit of a fright there, Dera. Come, will you help me draw water from the well?"

Dera nodded without looking up, and walked with a shaky gait towards the well. Scarlett's heart was heavy with guilt and pity for this poor child. She knew she had acquired a permanent shadow in the form of a silent, young girl. Dera took the bucket from Scarlett's hand and attached the handle to the hoist. Scarlett watched with a feeling of deep sadness as Dera lowered the bucket into the well. She wondered what was occupying the child's thoughts as she performed the mundane task with a surprising ease for her small, young frame.

As Dera retrieved the bucket from the well, Scarlett moved forward to unhook it from the hoist. Dera stepped quickly across her path and shot Scarlett a brief, almost undetectable glare. It was enough to stop Scarlett in her tracks.

A faint, cramp-like pain radiated inward from her scar, which turned quickly into a flood of apprehension. The blood of Phenoluh still clung to Dera, crusted and brownish. She looked, for a moment, almost inhuman. Scarlett stood aside as Dera moved past her, towards the cottage. This was truly a surreal moment for Scarlett and, no doubt, for the child as well.

It looked as though Dera was going to clean up the mess she had made by herself. Scarlett felt strangely redundant, as if she had changed places with Dera and was now the helpless child with nobody to turn to for solace. She could do nothing else but follow behind Dera and return to the house.

Once inside, Dera immediately went to work. Grabbing a large piece of material, she soaked it in the bucket and dropped to her knees, frantically scrubbing back and forward through the congealed blood. She only succeeded in spreading the mess to a larger area, frustrating her more as her movements became more erratic and somewhat violent. Scarlett made a monumental effort to fight back the tears, and knelt slowly beside Dera. She gently took the rag from the child's bloody hands. Dera let out a short, sharp scream of frustrated anguish, but released the cloth to Scarlett before falling in a heap onto the floor, crying uncontrollably. Scarlett began to mop up the blood from the outer perimeter of the mess, and worked her way inward towards the centre, leaving Dera to release her grief.

Perhaps an hour had passed, maybe longer, and the final traces of last night's tragedy were finally erased from the interior of the cottage. All that remained now was the trail from door to grave and, of course, Dera. She hadn't moved from her position - on her knees, sitting on her heels, with her face buried in her hands on the floor. Scarlett quietly left through the back door to remove any sign of Phenoluh's final journey, as Dera's little body trembled slightly. The morning mist now cleared and the sounds of day life, carrying across from Mills Wall, posed an element of risk for Scarlett as she quickly kicked and shuffled the loose dirt around. She was able to effectively cover the bloody trail quite easily and return to the cottage without detection. There were a small handful of townsfolk outside the walls going about their daily habits, but none chanced to look her way.

Dera still hadn't moved or changed position, and Scarlett sat down on the floor beside her, placing a gentle hand on the child's back.

"Dera, please, come with me?"

The child remained motionless.

"Please? We need to get cleaned up, and you need some new clothes. Let me fill the basin and I will come and fetch you."

Still no response. Scarlett stood and went to fill the wash basin, then realised she must risk another trip outside, to the well, for more water.

When she returned, Scarlett was horrified to find no sign of Dera. As she put the bucket down, she realised exactly where to find her, and headed straight out the back to where Phenoluh lay. Dera stood by her mother's makeshift graveside and gazed silently towards town. It was as if someone had called out to her, and she was trying to see who it was. This sent a jolt through Scarlett, not unlike the feeling of falling out of bed on the cusp of sleep. The sight of a young girl, covered in stale blood, would be enough to erupt the entire countryside into a hysteria that would make the panic in the marketplace seem like a funeral service.

"Quickly, inside! We must not be seen!"

Dera turned slowly, looked at Scarlett for a moment, then at her feet as she shuffled to the door like a marionette on strings.

Chapter 5

With a loud groan, then a choking gasp, Joshua woke suddenly and sat bolt upright on his bed. He had fallen asleep fully clothed on top of the covers. He hadn't even removed his shoes. The last thing Joshua remembered before falling into a fitful slumber was sitting on the end of his bed, staring at the floor in misery and shame. There was no time to indulge in his self-pity now. He had what seemed an impossible task to perform, and now only two days to succeed. Failure would most likely result in his death.

His sleep had been troubled with vague but terrible dreams. Broken visions of the demon woman advancing upon him, with gleaming blade in hand. He also faintly recalled a small, dark, shadowy figure behind the witch, off to the left of her. The figure seemed to be watching intently, like a morbid witness to his execution.

Shaking off the remnants of sleep, Joshua struggled to his feet and stretched lazily. He let out another groan and stumbled out of his room to the staircase. The small, dark figure was undoubtedly a young girl. He fancied it even reminded him of the mute girl who lived by the forest, outside of town. Every morning, she would come into town with her mother, who would haul a small cart filled with bundles of kindling to sell at the market. The child would always be running ahead of her mother, who constantly called out to her to slow down and mind the townsfolk. Could this be a portent? An omen of sorts? She was certainly a lively child...

The girl seemed healthy and strong, and lived away from town with only her mother. Her silent tongue would also be an added bonus to the traders. Joshua was filled with a sudden excited urgency. Having chosen his target, he now rushed downstairs to check on the remaining three children in his cellar, detouring past the pantry to fetch them some food. A small loaf of bread, a small tub of lard, and a pitcher of water would suffice for the time being. The children hadn't eaten for more than a day, and Joshua wanted neither to starve nor spoil them.

Pellegrin Melkerin glared at Joshua disapprovingly from his portrait in the hall, as he put the food on a small table and shifted the corner to reveal the lever. As the door swung inwards, quiet sobs echoed up the stairwell. He quickly picked up the children's breakfast and rushed to the top of the stairs.

"Shut up!" he barked in a forced whisper and the crying ceased instantly. "Stand up. I want to have a look at you. I have brought you food..."

Obediently, the children rose, moved towards the centre of the room, and stood side by side. Joshua placed the tray on the stone floor, and then proceeded to give the children his usual examination. All the while, three sets of hungry eyes fixed themselves upon the meagre feast on the floor. Satisfied by what he saw, Joshua turned and left the children without a word, as they fell upon the tray like vultures.

The three children ate in silence. Their eyes had become accustomed to the total darkness, somewhat, though they still had to function primarily by feel, as they shared the food amongst themselves. The dry, chewy bread had begun to turn stale and the lard had a peculiar smell to it, but they wolfed it down greedily nonetheless. The eldest, twelve year old Peter Menser, finally broke the silence.

"Poor Ander. I wonder how he's faring..."

Gilda Sween cleared her throat, began to say something, then thought better of it and continued to finish her mouthful. The nine year old didn't want to say what she was thinking. It was a thought that children her age should not be entertaining.

"Do you think maybe he has gone back home?" Ellie Horace spoke up.

Also nine years old, Ellie had lived a sheltered life. Her parents fussed over her incessantly and spoiled her at every chance they got. Of the three remaining children, the last few days had been hardest on her. Gilda had taken it upon herself to comfort Ellie, who spent the most part in tears, pining for her mother and father. Gilda was the oldest of five children, and prided herself on mothering her younger siblings while her parents worked in the community garden.

"I fear he is dead," said Gilda, then instantly wished she hadn't spoken her mind. Ellie burst into tears and scrambled back over to the corner of the room, closely followed by Gilda.

"Ellie, I'm so sorry. I'm most likely completely wrong. Don't fret. I'm sure we will all be able to go home again soon."

"No, we won't. We're going to die. Just like Ander!" said Ellie between sobs.

Gilda put her arms around her friend to comfort her. "Don't speak like that, Ellie. Don't think like that! We *will* get out of here! Now, come back and finish your meal or Peter may eat your share."

Peter didn't say another word. He shared Gilda's initial opinion, and had to summon every ounce of courage he could muster to prevent himself from breaking down like Ellie. As hopeless and doomed as their situation seemed, he would be damned if he was going to let these young girls see him fall to pieces. Peter continued to eat in silence, as tears fell down his cheeks in the dark.

* * *

Dera sat, deep in thought, as Scarlett gently, and in silence, wiped the caked blood from the child's tiny body. Her playmates still hadn't shown their faces. Not since The Sacred Blade Of Profanity had announced its presence. They kept strictly to the shadows within the places in Dera's mind that she had yet to gather the courage and necessary strength to explore.

"I hope you are ok," Dera spoke within. *"I will come for you when I am able."*

... Nothing.

The sun now risen above the trees, dawn had become day, as the townsfolk went about their daily business, completely oblivious to the slaughter that had occurred so close by. Scarlett began to feel uneasy. They had spent far too long in the cottage, and at any given moment a neighbour could come visiting. The escape route already mapped out in her head, Scarlett would take Dera out the back way, past Phenoluh's resting place, and into the dense forest. As Dera tied her shoes, Scarlett glanced out the window, towards Mills Wall. Three people seemed to be making their way in the direction of the cottage.

"Dera, we have to leave now! Quick. Take only what you need."

The child immediately sprang into action, running to the far end of the room. She returned with a small, round mirror, nodding solemnly at Scarlet. They quickly slipped out the back of the cottage, and into the woods. Phenoluh would be discovered before long, as, no doubt, the mother and child would be missed in the marketplace this morning.

Scarlett and Dera needed to put as much distance between themselves and the grisly scene as they could, in as short a time as possible.

Before they entered into the trees, Dera stopped to say a final farewell to her mother's corpse. She felt remorse, but she didn't really miss her for some strange reason. In fact, every memory she had of Phenoluh began to disappear from her mind, one by one.

Chapter 6

Dera stared at the semi-concealed remains of Phenoluh, who was quickly becoming a random stranger to the disturbed child. The Sacred Blade Of Profanity had touched her, just as it had touched Scarlett so many centuries past.

"We must go, Dera," Scarlett said anxiously. This was so out of character for her. Time and the consequences to others had always been the least of Scarlett's concerns. It was as if this aloof young child had stolen something indiscernible from her, taken her edge. Dera seemed to walk with a new air of confidence, while Scarlett felt heavy and strangely worried. About what? She couldn't figure it out.

One thing that was undeniable in her mind, was that because of her incompetence and carelessness, she had given a child over to a corruption of the soul that will never be reversed. Dera now walked with a slight skip in her step, which mocked Scarlett for some unknown reason. Unbeknownst to her, Dera had been reunited with her silent, invisible friends. She was no longer alone. Scarlett, on the other hand, had never felt such desolation.

A terrible jealousy took Scarlett as her eyes fell upon the back of the oblivious little girl. Her hand moved of its own accord to rest on the handle of the insidious Blade Of Power , and Scarlett shamefully caught herself plotting the slaughter of her new ward.

What is happening to me? This child has taken something from me. The Blade Of Power can get it back.

The Sacred Blade pulsed beneath Scarlett's hand with morbid glee at the thoughts she was entertaining. Just as suddenly as it began, the excited throb ceased. The Sacred Blade Of Profanity anticipated Scarlett's next thought – a thought sparked by its very own bloodthirsty impatience.

Scarlett knew what had to be done. Only one can possess The Sacred Blade at any given time.

Has my time come to pass? she pondered. The part of her that wished for it to be so... The quiet. Rest. Peace at long and final last...

That part began to grow. It began to spread, slowly, but with malign purpose, stirring the ever decreasing part of her psyche that craved and lusted after The Blade, to claw back at the crushing nothingness that threatened to envelop her.

"Dera, slow down a moment. We must head towards the city of Eve. It's this way." Dera slowed her bouncing trot, glancing over her shoulder in the direction Scarlett had indicated, and nimbly changed her course.

Chapter 7

    Joshua entered the already bustling marketplace, just shy of the seventh hour. Several of the stallholders busily finished their setting up. Most of them were already trading, bargaining, and bartering. Only two remained unattended. Mr. Tilly, the merchant of fine headwear, had collected his misplaced stock and left for home in a huff. He had decided to wait until morning, and then close for the day as he sorted through his many hats to find which ones were rubbish and which were redeemable.

    The other, of course, was Phenoluh's modest stall of firewood and kindling. She had always made enough to meet the frugal needs of herself and her precious daughter. With the added benefits of the town's thriving bartering system, Phenoluh, and indeed all of the residents of Mills Wall and its surrounding folk, lived without want, let alone need. It was a prosperous town, as it was situated centrally on the land. Mills Wall was accessible from every direction, although Mellowood Forest, which flanked to the South, South-East, and stretched for nearly one hundred miles deep, was a strenuous and formidable choice of direction from which to approach.

    Joshua, in the many decades he had resided here, had not once set foot outside The Southern Gate. He had no real reason to. All that was out that way were the scattered homes and farms of a few, and a hell of a lot of trees. Joshua just never had reason until now. He was well aware that the mother and child lived through that gate. It now seemed very odd to Joshua that today would be the first time he will have crossed this boundary. Phenoluh and Dera's absence was already starting to cause a bit of a stir at the market. Anything out of the ordinary now put all of the townsfolk on edge, given recent events.

    As Joshua decided to get the jump on everyone and investigate first, that damned feeling of dread once again filled his being. Mildly confused, he rushed out of the market and onward to The Southern Gate. What had happened to Dera when she first brought The Sacred Blade Of Profanity into her home was now taking control of Joshua. Only, where the exciting horror fixed Dera to the spot, Joshua was compelled toward the southern end of town.

Trembling on the inside, almost uncontrollably, Joshua's frantic stumble gave the appearance of the top half of his body moving faster than his legs could take him. Unable to halt his stride, the terror began to claw its way in. He began to make involuntary sounds from the violent trembling and feeble attempts to cry out.

*** * ***

"Scarlett. The child has tasted blood. Innocence, irredeemable. You do know, should Dera take me in her hand again, all will be lost. She will take your life, as she did her poor mother. The girl will carry out my legacy and do my will. Your time on this plane will cease."

The monotone voice of The Sacred Blade Of Profanity pressed on, much to Scarlett's rapidly increasing annoyance.

"We have history, Scarlett, you and I. You know me just as I know you. She is a child, Scarlett. Small, young and frail, Scarlett. Yes, I can mould her and guide her to our mutual benefit, but you... You, Scarlett are infinitely more capable than this child. You know implicitly what is needed to maintain our Power and continuity. Our very existence!"

The Blade Of Power spoke a very persuasive truth. Scarlett, weighted heavily by the incredible burden The Sacred Blade was lavishing on her, walked stiffly. It was as if she would at any moment tear away, either left or right, and continue to run until she would fall dead. She could only trudge onward, however. The Blade still pressed cruelly on her lung - a pointed reminder of Scarlett's mortality.

"Put your hand around me, Scarlett. You do not want to lose me to Dera."

Despite Scarlett's best efforts, and completely against her will, her hand moved smoothly and easily over the pommel, her slender fingers closing like a slow motion wave around the elaborate handle. The horrible taste of bile crept up into her throat as the compelling voice continued.

"Come, Scarlett... Easy prey, this one.... Just a single strike. Down the neck, Scarlett.... Come now. I have had my fill for the time being and am rightly sated. This is simple necessity. You must do it, Scarlett. You have no choice, Scarlett!"

Scarlett took a split moment to wonder if The Sacred Blade Of Profanity was actually beginning to panic. The voice grew louder and slightly strained, as the taunts and prods threatened to escalate into something much, much worse.

* * *

Passing through The Southern Gate, Joshua felt faint and dizzy. He didn't, or couldn't, slow his frantic gait, however. His innards threatened to expel themselves from his dry mouth, and sweat stung his eyes, as a multitude of thoughts scrambled at once to be heard.

This must be what Death feels like.

The dominant thought beat against the inside of his skull as he stumbled, mechanically across the fields, towards the cottage by the woods.

Word of the unusual absence of mother and daughter had spread fast. The entire town now congregated in the marketplace to throw around wild theories of what may have come to pass. Joshua's thoughts seemed to come well after his actions, and he realised his movements had shifted from a panic-stricken race toward the cottage, to the laborious trudging of a feeble old man. His steps were now a mimicry of Phenoluh's terrifying last march to her doom, as he neared the scene of perhaps the most brutal slaughter ever witnessed by the town of Mills Wall.

Joshua was a total wreck by the time he reached the gate to Phenoluh's home. The bloodlust energy hung thickly in the air around the cottage as he passed through the gate. He barely had his wits about him as he stumbled to the door, which hung slightly ajar. The apprehension achieved complete dominance over him, as he nervously and fearfully, knocked on the jamb.

* * *

The conversation was cheerful and light-hearted. Dera's friends, who, incidentally, she knew as The Prii, could do nothing in defence against The Sacred Blade Of Profanity. Its Power, in contrast to The Prii, was absolute. The fetid stench of ancient blood and shrieks of psychic terror sent The Prii fleeing in dismay to the safe darkness of Dera's 'inner sanctum', leaving their grief stricken and soul shaken friend to fend off the onslaught of The Blade alone.

Even once back in the hands of Scarlett, The Prii dared not leave the safety of their hiding place. Being the complete antithesis of the profane, they easily eluded The Sacred Blade. Something had called to them from the inexplicable reaches of this realm. Not a voice, per se - more a signal or tune of sorts. This calling filled The Prii with a surge of joyous Power, reassuring them it was safe to return. Dera was eager, if not desperate, to be reunited with her friends. Now they were back, and they brought with them the familiar fine mood and laughter that she so greatly needed. This gave Dera strength, and drove the dark clouds of fear and confusion back into the void.

Scarlett, on the other hand, was deeply involved in a one-sided conversation which was far from cheerful. The Sacred Blade Of Profanity was indeed showing signs of panic. Its voice was now taking on a shrill, demented tone as the Blade continued to plead its case. Scarlett's hand began to cramp as her grip involuntarily tightened around the handle. She knew from much experience that her iron clad will was still no match for the will of The Blade. She had the scars to remind her. Slowly, gradually, and despite Scarlett's most valiant efforts, The Blade began to lift from its sheath.

What The Sacred Blade Of Profanity wants… The Sacred Blade Of Profanity invariably gets.

"Stop!"

Scarlett's voice echoed among the trees and Dera froze in her tracks, turning back to Scarlett with a grimace. As the child began to rejoin her new mentor, Scarlett forcefully dropped to her hands and knees, The Sacred Blade Of Profanity now fully drawn and held down on the mossy ground. Scarlett looked up at Dera as she cautiously approached.

She glared at Dera, her eyes filled with a hellish blaze as she attempted to remain on all fours. The now delirious Blade of Power, however, had more sinister ideas developing within its malice-driven intent. Only then did Dera realise that The Prii had once again fled, so swiftly and silently, she was confused as to how long they had been gone. Time seemed to stand still for Dera—or was it moving backwards? The poor child had no comprehension of what was happening at that moment. Her little feet carried her forward, yet she seemed to be as rooted to the spot as the surrounding trees.

Scarlett shakily rose onto one foot as she struggled to remain down.

"Get...Away...From...Me!!"

The guttural roar that escaped from Scarlett was enough to shake Dera from her trance-like state. In an incomprehensible terror, she turned and fled blindly into the surrounding forest. As she tore through the trees, an agonised scream reached Dera's ears. She wanted to turn back. She knew the scream had come from Scarlett. At that moment, The Prii returned in force and begged Dera to stay on her current course. They didn't communicate through voice, but by a combination of musical sounds and colourful images. The tunes that resonated through her body now were of fear. The colours that flooded her vision, greyish brown and murky.

In nine years The Prii had not once led Dera astray. This time, she was convinced, was no different. The scream she heard was followed by silence. Dera continued to run as The Prii urged her onwards. Once they saw that Dera paid heed to their pleas, The Prii gradually softened their tone. Colour returned to Dera's vision, and she slowed her pace to a comfortable trot. Eventually, Dera slowed again to a hurried walk. Without warning, the events of the past twelve hours or so suddenly crashed down around the bewildered child, and she fell to the ground, shivering with fear and the desolate reality of her situation.

* * *

"Hello? Ma'am? Are you home? You and the young one have been missed in town this morning."

Joshua was met with a morbid silence that screamed louder than the crowd after yesterday's tragedy. Pushing the door open, he peered inside to find the place empty. One thing, however, didn't escape his attention - the familiar smell of blood. Scarlett seemed to have efficiently removed any physical trace of the murder, but Death lingered in the air, assaulting Joshua's already befuddled senses. He knew the scent of Death well. He had been around it, and indeed party to it, more than anybody was aware. But this was different.

Joshua knew, all at once, that The Blade was at the centre of whatever had happened here. Although the idea filled him with apprehension, Joshua had also become strangely calm. His innards now ceased their spasmodic trembling, and he was actually able to formulate a coherent thought. Joshua knew The Sacred Blade Of Profanity was far from this place, and was highly unlikely to be returning anytime soon.

What had happened here? Joshua pondered. *The place is left spotless, but surely there must be a corpse?*

He went back out through the front door with a new sense of purpose.

"If that damn witch has killed the girl, there will be hell to pay!"

Joshua rushed straight to the well. Peering down into the darkness proved a futile affair, so he hollered down to, hopefully, a survivor. Preferably the mute.

"Hello!"

He waited for the booming echo to cease, and listened for any sounds or response, but to no avail. Moving to the perimeter, Joshua began making his way to the trees out back.

Chapter 8

Scarlett had passed out from the pain. In order to let Dera escape a most certain Death that Scarlett wanted no part of, she had violently driven The Sacred Blade down into her risen thigh.

Now, Scarlett slept. It was a deep and unusually peaceful sleep. The Sacred Blade Of Profanity was very satisfied with this outcome. The child was all alone now, or so the insidious Dagger believed. The Blade remained in the possession of the more suited of the two, Scarlett.

"Oh, Scarlett, Scarlett..." The Blade gloated to its deranged self. *"What have we gone and done to ourselves now?"*

All the while, Scarlett slumbered, unaware as The Blade continued its private celebration. More than a hundred consecutive kills would still pale to insignificance when matched against the pain-sweetened blood of its host. This could never be a regular occurrence; otherwise The Sacred Blade Of Profanity would choose to feed on no other. This, of course, would be detrimental to the same degree for them both. One could not thrive without the other and, ultimately, one could not survive without the other.

As Scarlett slept, Dera lay not two miles to her West. She knew the forest immediately surrounding her home like she knew her own face, but this part of Mellowood was unfamiliar. Her normally keen sense of direction had eluded her. The girl was lost.

She had spent many hours over the years studying every line, every curve, and blemish, every expression she could create on her visage. In choosing not to talk, her small round mirror was a very handy and precious tool. Given to Phenoluh by Dera's father just before he passed away, Phenoluh thought it was pretty, but didn't find much use for it. Except, maybe to entertain Dera with when she was very young. Of course, she had kept the mirror - it was a sentimental gift - the last gift her beloved Michael had presented her with before being so suddenly snatched from her life.

Dera had become very attached to the mirror. It made communication and interaction with The Prii much more clear and unencumbered. She had already long ago realised the connection between The Prii and this mysterious mirror, though its true purpose was yet to be revealed to her. Dera took it from her pocket as she lay on the soft grass, held it to her heart, and cried for her mother until she too fell into a deep sleep.

* * *

Upon reaching the back of the cottage, Joshua instantly noticed what Scarlett believed to be a thorough concealment of the trail from door to grave. In her haste, and amid the several distractions that plagued her mind during the course of the previous night, Scarlett had made a terrible error in judgement. Her dominant concept of time, as afforded to her by The Sacred Blade, had been turned on its head. Up until that point, Scarlett had no problem perceiving time and space as malleable. When necessary, she would effortlessly move 'sideways in time', giving her the ability to assess situations without the interference of the mundane, 'agreed upon' reality of time and space. With The Ritual Of Cleansing looming, this was no longer so. The Blade Of Power was becoming erratic, and Scarlett was fast losing control over its every whim. Functioning in such linear fashion had long since become alien to her. What Scarlett now conceived about matters of time was that it was short, and it would not bend to her will, as she was so accustomed. Panic and undue haste leading to the inevitable result....

Joshua slowly walked the several steps to where Phenoluh lay. Even Scarlett's hurried burial of Phenoluh was clearly evident. So much to the point that Joshua knew at once the child did not lie there, unless, perhaps, it was a shallow grave for two. As he bent to inspect Scarlett's handiwork more closely, Joshua realised just how much of a rush she had been in to conceal the body. With a simple brush of his hand, he partially revealed Phenoluh's mutilated corpse. Minimal effort on his behalf fully revealed that the makeshift grave housed only one. It was a frustrated relief.

Where the hell was the girl?

Joshua followed the trail back to the door, and once again entered the cottage. Maybe a clue was overlooked on his initial inspection of the scene. Phenoluh's murder looked absolutely horrific. Joshua shuddered at the notion that this could very well have been him. It very likely still may be. This was definitely not the way Joshua wished to leave this world.

Standing on the very spot where Phenoluh had fallen, Joshua slowly set his gaze around the humble cottage, essentially one large room. His squinting eyes came to rest on the large bed that Scarlett had awoken on, situated near the far end of the cottage. Joshua made his way across the room. Stopping just short of the bed, he saw the bloody result of yet another oversight on Scarlett's behalf—the bedding was generously smeared with blood. As Joshua observed the heinous evidence, he swore he heard a sinister chuckle, but couldn't identify with certainty whether it came from inside, outside, or even from within his own head.

The Sacred Blade Of Profanity chuckled to itself as Scarlett lay unconscious for the second time in less than a day. It watched Joshua as he continued to discover Scarlett's mishaps. The Blade watched with an intense hunger, which was building once again. This, despite a very satisfying night of gluttony, followed by a hearty breakfast treat provided by its most generous host.

The self-awareness of The Sacred Blade Of Profanity was something one would consider extraordinary, even ridiculous. The fact that it 'sees', with time and space offering no restriction would certainly be deemed preposterous….

Perhaps, the idea is not so absurd. But in the case of The Blade Of Power there were definite restrictions imposed. Indeed, such restrictions were imbued in The Sacred Blade Of Profanity at the time of its crafting.

Unbeknownst to everyone involved - even The Blade - was The Watcher…Void. It was the Ancient witness that followed The Blade on its endless journey. Spanning centuries, traversing worlds and incomprehensible planes of existence as it passes from host to unwitting host. The connection between Watcher and Blade was weakening by the moment. The Ritual Of Cleansing must be performed before the next dark moon gave way to the new. In failing this, the link would be forever broken, as would any control over The Sacred Blade Of Profanity.

This would bring about catastrophic circumstances, both in the illusive here and now, as well as anywhere The Blade had ever been. It would also create a disturbing ripple where it may yet appear... throwing the agreed upon order of time and space into a chaotic mayhem.

The Sacred Blade was unaware of this possible outcome, but knew without question something very inauspicious loomed. A sense of impending freedom permeated the air, though The Blade found this concept difficult to fully comprehend. Its creation, its purpose, and certainly its continued existence, was one of servitude and reward. True freedom... the freedom this sinister and bloodhungry Dagger witnessed around it consistently, seemed naught but an unattainable fantasy.

* * *

Meanwhile, only a couple of miles away, Dera rolled onto her back and slowly opened her eyes. The late morning sun flashed intermittently through the moving leaves above her as Dera squeezed her eyes shut and struggled to sit up. The mysterious mirror sat by her side. It seemed to be calling to Dera, reflecting the dancing sunlight back up into her downturned face. She picked up the mirror and turned it several times around in her hands thoughtfully, before peering deeply into her own searching eyes.

The Prii remained silent in the shadows of Dera's mind. They knew not to interfere when Dera connected with The Mirror. Her gaze began to sharpen and shrink to a point between her eyes.

"Oh, Mother...Please forgive me..."

The world dissolved around Dera and she found herself walking hand in hand with Phenoluh. A long forgotten memory triggered by The Mirror, though it had occurred only two summers previously. It was a memory of the time Dera had pounded some respect into an older boy. Phenoluh had pulled her off the poor lad, whose eyes were both swollen shut and painfully afflicted with a front tooth left poking through his upper lip.

Dera remembered thinking *That'll teach you to pick on girls, you coward,* as her secretly proud mother led her away through town, towards home... Home...

Maybe, this had been a terrible dream. Maybe Phenoluh was waiting for her back at the cottage, a hot meal of her favourite venison stew simmering away. Dera realised she was actually quite ravenous. The realisation brought her instantly back to where she sat. The Prii came forward to comfort Dera, their soothing melodies blanketing her in a soft, bluish hue. They successfully hid their concern for their deeply troubled and dear friend.

Dera decided to return home. The reality of what she had done was too prevalent to convincingly dream otherwise. She did not know where else to go. She stood and brushed herself off. Still clutching the mirror in her little hand, Dera tried to get her bearings. She turned slowly in a complete circle, then again in the opposite direction. It was in that moment The Prii gently stopped her—she faced the direction of the cottage. With an encouraging nudge, The Prii set Dera into motion. She placed the mirror safely in her pocket and raced off through the forest.

* * *

Astra Kirltth sat with a wrinkled brow of concentration, gazing intently at the randomly scattered grains of sand.

Scarlett has fallen to The Sacred Blade Of Profanity, leaving the very fabric of existence exposed and balancing precariously on twisted lines. I must find Scarlett and The Blade while time still exists.

As this thought occurred, a moth fluttered into her line of vision, coming to rest on the sand between Astra's scrying hands.

The Moth... The Bringer Of Knowledge 'sees' Astra's thoughts -and intent-, then vanishes.

* * *

Joshua wished fervently that he had an assistant of sorts. Better yet, several assistants. His line of work would never allow him such a luxury. Secrecy, and its accompanying loneliness, was Joshua's lot, self-inflicted through selfishness and greed. The Sacred Blade Of Profanity had been biding its time over several years with Joshua's ultimate fate. Just as you or I would sit down to a delicious meal and breathe it in... we close our eyes and savour the smell, then open them, and imagine how it's going to taste. Now, consider the ageless Blade Of Power. Several years, being but the deep breath and hungry gaze before you or I would gratefully devour our bounty.

Joshua carefully covered Phenoluh's corpse more thoroughly than he had found her. He had also hidden the bloodstained bedding underneath the bed itself, as he concluded it best that nobody else from the nosy town of Mills Wall discover what had transpired. As he stood back to inspect the burial, Joshua was satisfied. Now the problem was, did Joshua risk all for one? If he didn't, the deal was automatically off, and he had been paid handsomely in advance for four children.

The traders were a ruthless lot. Their leader, Jahl-Rin, was rumoured to be a cannibal, amongst other diabolical traits. Joshua never failed to deliver, whether it be stolen artefacts, a "lost" cargo, or a child or four whose whereabouts fast became unknown, even to Joshua. This put him in good standing with Jahl-Rin and his like. Although, just as with this contract, he was always plagued by mishaps every step of the way. It was worth the money he was paid, however. He'd had many dealings with Jahl-Rin and his crew. A healthy mix of fear and respect always got him through unscathed and significantly more well off.

Mellowood Forest was such an insanely vast amount of ground to cover, and Joshua agreed with himself that it would be a fruitless venture in trying to find the girl.

He did have four... he still had three. Joshua decided to return home to his remaining captives.

Maybe the child will come back in search of her mother, thought Joshua as he glanced towards the town. He began walking away from the cottage slowly and then stopped.

In that moment, Joshua questioned his heretofore leisurely pace, then exclaimed "Dammit! I'm running out of time!" to no-one in particular, as he began rushing back to Mills Wall as fast as his bulk would carry him.

* * *

An unfamiliar destination, though she has been here many times. A descent into a higher realm. A paradox in time and space... as vast and cavernous as the skull space of the fallen sparrow. Lurking within this miniscule expanse, Scarlett feels strongly in her element. Here and now, she can make any and every thought or whim become manifest in the world of form.

But Scarlett has ceased to care.

The past few years in that world had been particularly hard on her. A steadily advancing loss of control over the desires of The Sacred Blade Of Profanity had exhausted her, culminating in this most recent and devastating tragedy. All that Scarlett desires, she has, right in the true here and now.

Open and free, to swallow all but nothing. Closed to this world, Scarlett falls into its embrace… the infinitesimal point of infinite space.

The End...

Of The Beginning...

Epilogue

...Scarlett is closed to this world, leaving Astra Kirltth with very little to go by. Only the direction - South East. Astra, however, has lost the connection with Scarlett and The Blade Of Power. Her knowledge of Mellowood Forest is exemplary and her affinity with the Spirit of Mellowood has earned her the wisdom of its countless secrets. She has only the direction though. Not the distance. It will expend every portion of her energy to succeed, but Astra Kirltth must find them before it is too late.

Dera begins to recognise her surroundings and instantly picks up the pace. Skipping over and around rocks, hurdling familiar fallen trees, Dera sprints through the forest.

Her well-trained lungs breathe calmly and easily. She doesn't even break a sweat. Dera Harke has no idea why she is running so intently, back to that strange woman who lay dead behind her home.

Meanwhile, Joshua has returned home to find two more sick children and a cellar that reeks of vomit, faeces and urine. Exasperated, Joshua flies into a psychopathic rage. Ellie's screams, as Joshua grabs her roughly by the hair, stab like needles through Peter's ears. Hiding in the opposite corner, beneath the stairs, he cowers and watches as Joshua drags the hysterical girl back and forth across the room, babbling inanities which are interrupted by bouts of sobs and growling yells. Peter remains petrified in the shadows. Poor Gilda lays shivering in her own vomit, not completely aware of what is taking place.

The Sacred Blade Of Profanity greedily taps the powerful flow that passes through Scarlett, deep into the earth and deep into space. Into infinity. The realm Scarlett inhabits is akin to a vast conduit. A multiple crossroad of possibilities that become reality with the purity of a mere single minded thought.

Right here… right now… Scarlett feels maybe its best she thinks nothing at all…

Just… Be…

Made in the USA
Columbia, SC
14 April 2017